SUPERHUMAN SPEED

Jessica Rusick

Big Buddy Books

An Imprint of Abdo Publishing
abdobooks.com

abdobooks.com

Published by Abdo Publishing, a division of ABDO, PO Box 398166, Minneapolis, Minnesota 55439. Copyright © 2022 by Abdo Consulting Group, Inc. International copyrights reserved in all countries. No part of this book may be reproduced in any form without written permission from the publisher. Big Buddy Books™ is a trademark and logo of Abdo Publishing.

Printed in the United States of America, North Mankato, Minnesota
102021
012022

THIS BOOK CONTAINS RECYCLED MATERIALS

Design: Emily O'Malley, Mighty Media, Inc.
Production: Mighty Media, Inc.
Editor: Rebecca Felix
Cover Photographs: Shutterstock Images
Interior Photographs: Benoit DUCHATELET/Flickr, p. 27; Brandon Potts, p. 19l Eddie Codel/Flickr, p. 23; Shutterstock Images, pp. 5, 7, 9, 11, 13, 15, 17, 21, 25, 29
Design Elements: Shutterstock Images

Library of Congress Control Number: 2021942811

Publisher's Cataloging-in-Publication Data
Names: Rusick, Jessica, author.
Title: Superhuman speed / by Jessica Rusick
Description: Minneapolis, Minnesota : Abdo Publishing, 2022 | Series: Superhuman science | Includes online resources and index.
Identifiers: ISBN 9781532197031 (lib. bdg.) | ISBN 9781644947197 (pbk.) | ISBN 9781098219161 (ebook)
Subjects: LCSH: Human physiology--Juvenile literature. | Performance--Juvenile literature. | Motor ability--Juvenile literature. | Speed--Juvenile literature. | Super powers--Juvenile literature.
Classification: DDC 599.9--dc23

DON'T TRY THIS AT HOME

Many of the superhuman feats described in this book were overseen by trainers and doctors. Do not attempt to re-create these feats. Doing so could cause injury.

CONTENTS

AMAZING ABILITY

Superheroes have superpowers. But real men and women also have **amazing** abilities. Some people can move **incredibly** fast. They have superhuman speed!

Scientists say the human body can handle running at a top speed of 40 miles per hour (64 kmh). No human has reached this speed.

WHAT IS SPEED?

Speed is how fast something moves. Imagine you are walking at 3 miles per hour (5 kmh). This is your speed. Velocity is your speed and direction. You are walking north. So, your velocity is 3 miles per hour (5 kmh) north.

Measuring your velocity can tell you how quickly you will reach a location.

MOVING MUSCLES

Your muscles help **determine** how fast you are. Humans have two kinds. Fast-twitch muscles help you move quickly in short bursts. Slow-twitch muscles help you move slowly for longer.

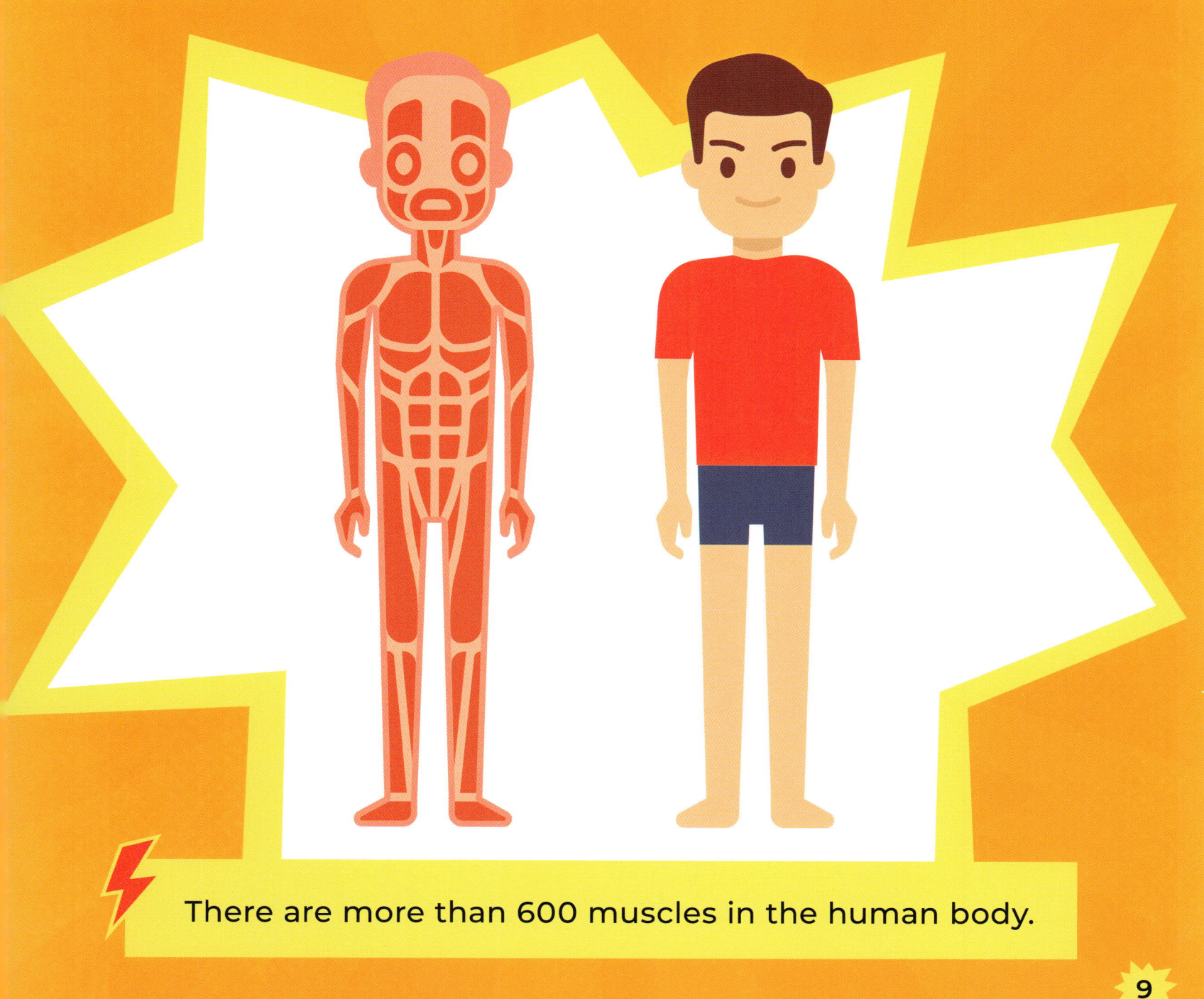

There are more than 600 muscles in the human body.

Fast-twitch muscles can reach **peak** force quickly. A force is a push or pull. It causes movement. For example, your feet push off the ground when you run. This **propels** you forward.

Runners often use starting blocks in races. These allow runners to start with extra force.

SKILLED SPRINTER

Fast-twitch muscles give you speed during **sprints**. Skilled sprinters raise their knees high and strike their feet down hard. This **propels** their bodies farther, faster.

Pumping your arms while running can increase your speed. When one arm moves quickly backward or forward, the body creates balance by quickly moving the opposite leg in the same direction.

Jamaican **sprinter** Usain Bolt is the fastest runner in the world. In 2009, he ran 100 meters in a record 9.58 seconds! Bolt's fast-twitch muscles **generate** lots of force. This **propels** him far with each step.

TOP SPEED

In 2009, Bolt reached a top speed of nearly 28 miles per hour (45 kmh).

Usain Bolt began running as a child. By age 12, he was the fastest runner at his school!

RAPID REACTION

Fast-twitch muscles also help you **react** fast! Imagine someone tosses you a ball. Your brain tells your hand to catch it. The time it takes your arm to move is your reaction time. Having stronger fast-twitch muscles results in a faster reaction time.

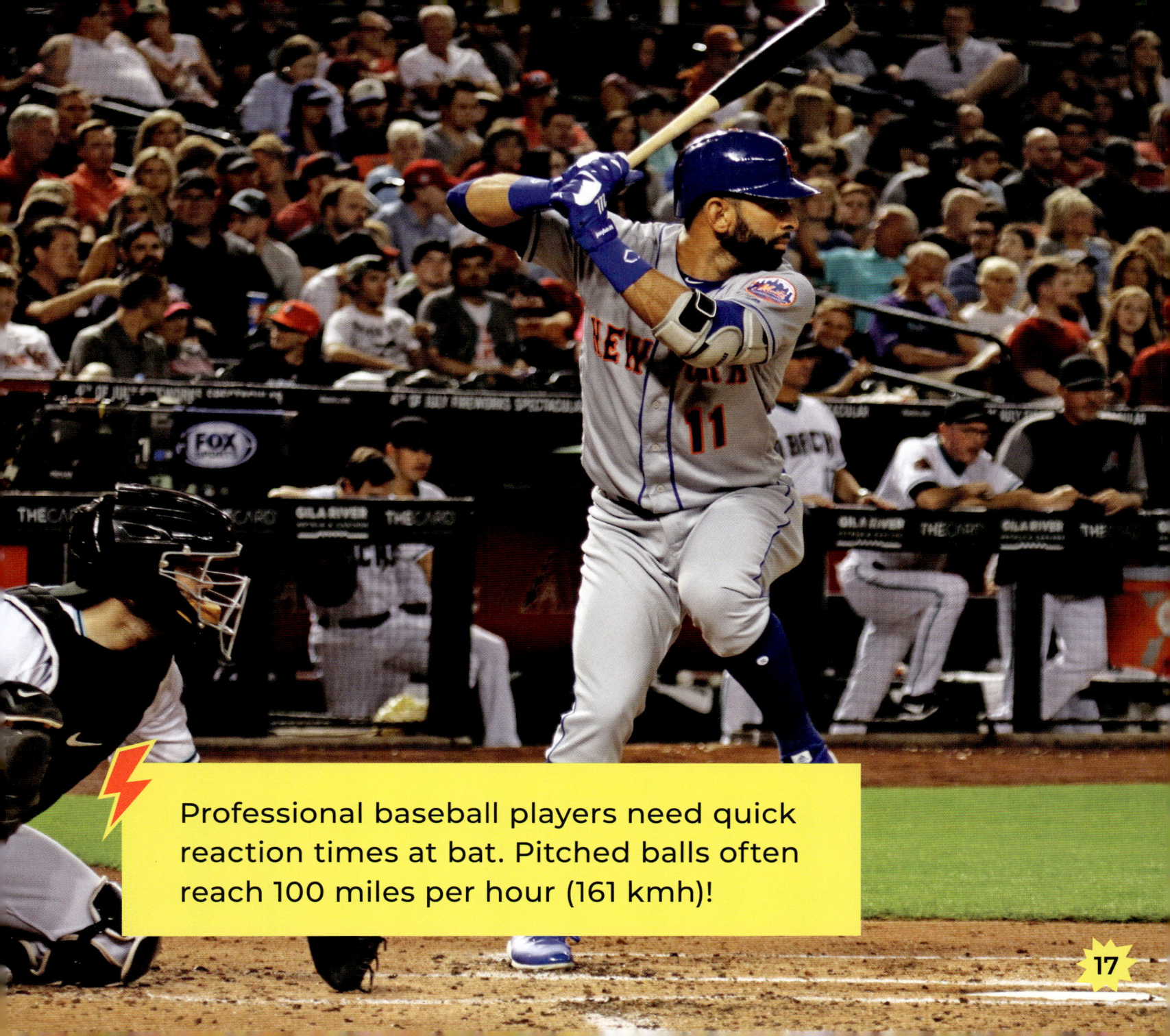

Professional baseball players need quick reaction times at bat. Pitched balls often reach 100 miles per hour (161 kmh)!

17

Anthony Kelly is an Australian **martial arts expert**. He has superhuman **reaction** times! In 2017, Kelly caught a tennis ball traveling 154 miles per hour (248 kmh). Kelly's fast-twitch muscles helped him catch the speeding ball.

Anthony Kelly moments before catching a speeding tennis ball

19

JET SPEED

Some people wear jet packs to reach superhuman speeds. Jet packs **propel** users with jets of gas or water. The jets create an upward force called lift and an outward force called thrust. These forces make jet pack wearers **soar** and speed through the sky!

Jet packs can be very costly to own! Many companies near bodies of water provide water jet pack rentals.

21

In 2016, British inventor Richard Browning **designed** a jet suit. It has several jet engines. In 2019, Browning flew his suit at more than 85 miles per hour (137 kmh). This broke a world record!

SUPERHERO

Browning is sometimes called the "real-life Iron Man."

Richard Browning hovers above cars in California.

#TAKEONGRAVITY

FAST FREE FALL

Some speedy humans are skydivers! **Gravity** pulls a skydiver toward Earth. This makes him fall at an increasing speed. Air pushes up against him, slowing him down. When these opposite forces become equal, the skydiver can't fall any faster. This speed is usually about 120 miles per hour (193 kmh).

Skydivers fall at different speeds depending on their weight and body position. Some diving partners hold hands so they fall at the same speed.

In 2012, Austrian Felix Baumgartner recorded the world's fastest skydive. Baumgartner dove from more than 24 miles (39 km) high. The air was very thin at that height. So, less air pushed on Baumgartner as he fell. At top speed, he fell at more than 843 miles per hour (1,357 kmh)!

Felix Baumgartner wore a protective suit during his record skydive. The outfit looked like a space suit!

BROAD JUMP

Want to improve your speed?
Try doing broad jumps!

1. Time how fast you can run a set distance.

2. Find an open space.

3. Set your feet shoulder-width apart.

4. Squat down and swing your arms back.

5. Jump forward as you swing your arms forward.

6. Perform these jumps several times each day to practice exerting force against the ground.

7. After one month, time yourself running the same distance as in step 1. Did your speed improve?

GLOSSARY

amazing—causing wonder or surprise.

design (dih-ZINE)—to make a plan for how something will appear or work.

determine—to be the cause of or reason for something.

expert—a person who has special skill or knowledge on a subject or activity.

generate—to create or produce something.

gravity—a natural force that pulls objects downward.

incredibly—in a way that is amazing or unbelievable.

martial arts (MAHR-shuhl artz)—Asian fighting arts, often practiced as sport. Karate and judo are martial arts.

peak—the highest point.

propel—to drive forward or onward by some force.

react—to act or feel a certain way when something happens. This action or feeling is called a reaction.

soar—to fly at great height by floating on air currents.

sprint—a run at top speed for a short distance. A sprinter is a person who does such a run.

ONLINE RESOURCES

Booklinks
NONFICTION NETWORK
FREE! ONLINE NONFICTION RESOURCES

To learn more about superhuman speed, please visit **abdobooklinks.com** or scan this QR code. These links are routinely monitored and updated to provide the most current information available.

INDEX